STO

FRIENDS
OF ACPL

ALLEN COUNTY PUBLIC LIBRARY

3 1833 00571

W9-DAZ-081

Stories of Regional America—some humorous, some filled with pathos—spotlight both the likes and differences of special peoples in colorful places. These peoples form the melting pot, which has become America. The action-filled accounts, each based on true fact, give the reader a deeper appreciation of his cultural background and a greater understanding of the peoples who have made his heritage possible.

The Famous Battle of Bravery Creek

BY LYNN HALL
ILLUSTRATED BY HERMAN B. VESTAL

GARRARD PUBLISHING COMPANY
CHAMPAIGN, ILLINOIS

PUBLIC LIBRARY
EORT WAYNE AND ALLEN COUNTY, IND.

Copyright © 1972 by Lynn Hall
All rights reserved. Manufactured in the U.S.A.
Standard Book Number: 8116–4253–4
Library of Congress Catalog Card Number: 78–163176

2124545

Contents

The Truth about Bravery Creek

Where did Bravery Creek get its name?

Orville Corcoran knew, because it was named in honor of his great-grandfather who was the hero of the battle fought there.

Johnnie Horsefeather knew, because *his* great-grandfather was the hero of that very same battle.

And Mr. Millering the historian knew, because he had Molly Corcoran's letters.

This is the story of how Bravery Creek got its name as told by these three men. Each man told the story as he had learned it, and each man believed that his story was the true one.

But as is often the case, the simple truth about Bravery Creek is not so very simple after all.

Orville Corcoran's Story

How Captain Corcoran Became a
Hero at Bravery Creek

In spite of its name, Bravery Creek is a very small stream, almost small enough to jump across if you get a running start. It ripples through the northeast corner of Iowa, from the Yellow River Forest to the Mississippi River.

On one still, hot August afternoon, four people sat on the bank of Bravery Creek. Four fishing lines pierced the surface of the water. There was no sound but the hum of mosquitos and the faraway roar of a tractor making hay.

Orville Corcoran had come fishing this afternoon because it was too hot to do anything else. He was a big bald man, wearing a pair of overalls with a label that said, "Oshkosh, B'Gosh." His farm was just beyond the creek.

Johnnie Horsefeather was there because he was an Indian, and he knew that this part of the creek was the best place to fish.

No one knew why the third man, Mr. Millering, had come. In fact no one knew much about Mr. Millering at all, except that he was in the Bravery Creek area to study local history. He was a young man in city clothes, and he looked rather out of place sitting on the creek bank.

The fourth fisherman was young Dennis, who had come fishing simply because he was ten years old and it was a hot summer afternoon. And besides, he liked to listen to Orville and Johnnie. He sat at the very edge of the bank with his feet in the water. It felt delicious, like chilly socks around his ankles.

"Sure is hot," Orville said, mopping his face with his shirt sleeve.

Johnnie Horsefeather snorted, "It's not so hot for this time of year."

Dennis waited for Orville and Johnnie to go on. He knew they would soon find something to argue about. They always did, and usually their arguments were interesting.

After a while Johnnie said, "The creek is high for August. That's why we catch no fish today."

"The creek's low," Orville growled. "Any fool can see that. Ain't that right, Dennis?"

But Dennis didn't want to take sides. It spoiled the fun of listening. Instead, he tried to aim the conversation in another direction.

"Bravery Creek," he said thoughtfully. "It's got a funny name, hasn't it? Do you know where its name came from, Orville?"

Orville grinned. "Do I know? Course I know, boy. It was named after my great-grandpa, Captain Corcoran, who led the famous battle of Bravery Creek. He was the hero of the whole thing, and he told the story to my grandpa, who told it to my pa, who told it to me. And if you want, I'll tell it to you."

Johnnie Horsefeather snorted, "Don't listen to him, Dennis. It didn't happen the way he tells it. I can tell you the true story."

Mr. Millering said nothing, but he smiled as though he knew a funny secret.

Dennis said, "I'd like to hear it both ways. Tell yours first, please, Orville."

Johnnie Horsefeather leaned back against a

tree and closed his eyes to show that he wasn't going to listen.

Orville stuck his fishing pole in the mud, looked around at his audience, and began.

This is the story that Orville told:

Back in the time of my great-grandpa, the town was just a handful of log cabins huddled

around the creek. Folks hadn't even been there long enough to give the creek a name.

Great-grandpa was just a young feller at the time, but he'd already made such a name for himself as an Indian fighter that the president of the United States gave him the title of honorary captain. He was just about the bravest man on the prairies in his time, and back then a man had to be mighty fearless even to want to live on the frontier.

All the Indians around here respected the captain, because they knew his reputation as a fighter and as a fair man. So they didn't give the new settlers any trouble.

At least in the beginning they didn't. But then one day, trouble started.

It was a Monday morning and, as you know, on Monday mornings every woman in the world thinks she's got to wash clothes. I never could figure out why that was, but I guess women have been washing on Monday mornings since the world began.

So on this particular Monday morning, all the

14

settlers' wives bundled up their families' home-spuns and took them down to the creek to wash them. The women used soap they made them-selves of hog-fat renderings, and they used the rocks in the creek for scrub boards.

They were standing around out there, knee deep in creek water, rubbing and scrubbing and arguing among themselves just as fast as they rubbed and scrubbed.

Little Molly Corcoran, the captain's wife, said, "We've lived here for a month now, and we still haven't been able to agree on a name for this place. I don't know why we can't call it Corcoran's Creek, since it was my husband who brought us here, and since he's the head of the settlement."

But one of the other ladies, Mrs. Martin, said, "I just don't like the sound of 'Corcoran's Creek.' It doesn't have enough style. 'Martin Valley' would have a much nicer ring to it, don't you think?"

A third lady joined in, and a fourth, each with her own suggestion for a name.

Suddenly the fifth lady said, "Quit your arguing for a minute and look at the water. It's all muddy."

They stopped arguing and looked, and sure enough the water was as muddy as a rathole in a rain storm. Quick as they could, the ladies gathered up soggy armfuls of laundry and sloshed

16

over to the bank of the creek. They climbed
out and stood watching the creek water. It got
muddier and muddier.

"What are we going to do?" Mrs. Martin
wailed. "We can't wash our clothes in muddy
water, and it's Monday morning, so we have to
wash our clothes."

Molly Corcoran thought for a minute, then said, "Follow me. We'll walk upstream a ways and see if we can find out what's making the water so muddy."

The women marched along the creek bank, trying to talk themselves into feeling brave. But life on the frontier was so different from the way they had lived back in Cincinnati that almost everything here scared them at first.

They came around a bend and suddenly they stopped. Through the bushes they could see Indians, lots of them. They were riding their ponies back and forth through the creek, yelling and splashing and churning up the muddy creek bottom like windmills in a tornado.

The ladies turned and ran.

Molly went to find her husband, who was working with the other men building a corral. She was still shaking with fright when she told him what she had seen.

"This is a problem," the captain said. "We can't let the Indians get away with muddying our water. We need it badly, not just for washing but for drinking too. I'd better ride over and have a talk with the chief."

"Oh no, don't do that," Molly begged. "It's too dangerous. They might scalp you."

Bravely the captain said, "Molly, it has to be done, and I will do it."

So the next morning he rode to the Indian village. Chief Bird-in-Hand was sitting outside his teepee. As the captain got down from his horse, the other Indians began to make a circle around him. But he wasn't afraid.

"Chief," he said, "your men have been riding their ponies through the creek and making the water so muddy that my people can't use it. We need clean water, so would you please tell your men not to do it anymore?"

20

But the chief just folded his arms stubbornly across his chest and said, "We were here first."

The captain's eyes narrowed into little slits. He was being as firm as he could.

The chief's eyes narrowed into slits too, stubborn slits.

The captain folded his arms across his chest and stared down at the chief with all the firmness he could get into one look. The chief just stared back, looking more and more stubborn every minute.

For a long time they stood that way. Finally Captain Corcoran said, "Then I guess it's war."

The chief nodded.

"We will meet on the hill beside the creek, three days from now," the captain said, and again the chief nodded.

Captain Corcoran turned, got on his horse, and rode bravely through the circle of watching Indians. He was mad at their infernal stubbornness, and he meant to fight the best Indian war of his whole life.

All that day and the next, the settlers worked to get ready. They figured they'd be outnumbered by about twenty to one, so they hurried up and built a log fort on the very top of the hill. Then the men sat down to clean their muzzle loaders and plan their strategy.

On the night before the battle, the men put all the women and children into a spring wagon and sent them off to Fort Crawford, where they'd be safe. Then the men settled down to wait.

There were just six of them, and by rights they should have been scared silly, but they were six of the bravest men the good Lord ever made. Besides, they knew they had the best Indian fighter in the whole Iowa Territory to lead them—the fearless Captain Corcoran.

Well, sir, dawn came a-slipping out over the prairie, and those redskins came roaring and whooping up the hill to the fort. They commenced shooting, and the settlers commenced shooting back, and the battle was on.

They fought all morning. The settlers were outnumbered twenty to one, but they still were not afraid. They were all great shots, and Captain Corcoran was the best of the lot. Before long the creek was running red with blood.

Along about the middle of the day, Captain Corcoran gathered his men around him in the middle of the fort. "Men," he said, pointing at the sun directly overhead, "it's midday and we're just about out of ammunition. We'll wait till the sun goes down," he motioned toward the western horizon, "and then I'll see if I can't sneak out the back way and get help."

"But captain," one young fellow said, "where

are you going to find more ammunition? We brought every gun and every bit of powder and shot in the area when we came."

"That's true," Captain Corcoran said. "But I might be able to find something almost as good."

Well, sir, after the sun went down, the captain slipped out and disappeared into the woods behind the fort. He was gone all night, but just

as the sun was rising again, he came back. This time he was driving a buckboard and a team of galloping horses, and he pulled right up to the front of the fort practically under the Indians' noses.

The back of the wagon was piled high with what looked like about 200 rifles. A blanket covered the pile, but it was easy to see the long

stick-like shapes poking up under the blanket. The men inside the fort got the door open in a hurry, and the team and wagon clattered inside.

"Captain, captain, you've done it!" the men shouted. "You saved us for sure. Where in thunder did you find all those guns?"

Captain Corcoran jumped down from the wagon, panted for a minute till he'd caught his breath, and said, "Now don't get all up in a heaval till you see what we've got here."

With that, he threw back the blanket. On the wagon bed was a huge pile of broomsticks, pitchforks, hoe handles, and just plain old tree branches.

For a minute the men just stood and stared. Finally one of them blurted out, "Captain, those aren't guns. They're broomsticks!"

Captain Corcoran just grinned. "Tom, I know they're broomsticks. You know they're broomsticks. But do the Indians know they're broomsticks? No. What they saw was me driving in here with a load of something that looked like a mess of guns, and with a look on my face that made them think I had the world by the tail.

"And now, if you men are brave enough to carry it off, what those Indians are going to see is all of us charging out of here, right smack at them, whooping and yelling as if we know we've got them beat. We'll shoot off what little ammunition we've got left, just as if we had plenty more where that came from, which we don't, but they don't know that. Are you with me?"

The men looked at one another and at the wagonload of broomsticks, and one by one they said, "I'm with you, captain."

They got on their horses, held their breath, and, with Captain Corcoran in the lead, they opened the fort door and charged.

The Indians took one look at the men coming toward them. For a quick minute they thought about the wagonload of guns they had just seen going into the fort. They thought about the brave way the white men were galloping toward them, and they decided it was time to get out.

They headed back to their village just as fast as their ponies would go.

"It worked! It worked!" the captain's men shouted. "You're the bravest man in the whole Iowa Territory—in the whole world." They pounded him so hard and so excitedly that they cracked one of his ribs. Then they hoisted him to their shoulders and carried him back to his cabin, where they whooped and hollered all night long, celebrating.

By morning they were worn out from the fighting and the whooping, but they had all come to a decision. They were going to name this place Bravery Creek, in honor of Captain Corcoran and the greatest of all his Indian wars.

Johnny Horsefeather's Story

How Chief Bird-in-Hand Outwitted the Settlers at Bravery Creek

By the time Orville had finished, Dennis' eyes shone with excitement. He was no longer watching his fishing pole or thinking about how good the water felt around his ankles.

"That was some battle all right," he said. "You must be proud to have a great-grandpa like Captain Corcoran."

Johnnie Horsefeather had been silent for so long that when he finally did say something, Dennis jumped.

"Hah. White man speak with rubber tongue."

"What do you mean?" Dennis asked.

"I mean Orville was stretching the truth—that's what I mean. If you want to know the facts of the battle, I will tell you. After all, it was *my* great-grandfather, Chief Bird-in-Hand, who was the real hero."

"Yes, please tell us about it," Dennis begged. Orville turned his back to Johnnie and sat scowling into the distance.

Mr. Millering still smiled wisely and said nothing.

This is the story that Johnnie Horsefeather told:

When the white men first came to live beside our creek, my people didn't care much, one way or the other. They liked Private Corcoran. He was the leader of the settlers and a nice enough young man, although he wasn't much of a warrior. The white men tended to their own business and we tended to ours, and in that way we got along.

That is, we got along until the day the trouble started. It was a very hot day, so a few

of the braves took their ponies to the creek to drink. My people had always done this, for centuries.

The ponies began to drink, but suddenly big foamy slathers of soapsuds were floating down the creek toward them. The ponies were afraid. They had never seen white mountains floating on water before, and neither had the braves. The ponies bolted and ran, dumping off their riders, left and right. Even my great-grandfather, mighty warrior that he was, was taken by surprise. He fell off into the creek, and his dignity was injured.

It took the braves three days of walking in the hot sun to round up their ponies, and by the time they got back to their village, they were seeing red.

"It's all the white men's fault," one tired brave said. The others agreed.

That night the chief called a council of all the braves.

"Our ponies must have clean water to drink," he said. "I will go tomorrow and talk to the chief of the white men. I will tell him of our need, and we will make peace."

"Don't go," his squaw said, from her corner of the teepee. "I am afraid of the white men. They might kill you."

But Bird-in-Hand was famous for his bravery. He was not afraid of the white men, or of anything else. The next day he rode to the settlers' cabins.

Private Corcoran was sitting in front of his cabin when the chief rode up. They nodded to each other, then Bird-in-Hand spoke.

"Your people are making soapsuds in our creek, and our ponies can no longer drink the water. Without water our ponies will die."

But Corcoran just looked stubborn and said, "Find someplace else to water them. We need clean clothes."

The chief stood there, growing firmer and firmer. He crossed his arms across his chest and made his eyes into narrow slits of firmness.

Private Corcoran sat there, with his arms crossed stubbornly.

The chief grew firmer.

Corcoran grew more stubborn.

At last the chief said, "Then we must make war."

Private Corcoran looked frightened, but he nodded.

"In three suns," the chief said, "we will meet in battle on that hill." He pointed to the hill beside the creek. Then without another word, he rode away.

He went back to his village and began making plans for the battle. Ours was a very small tribe at that time, with only the chief and twelve braves. And of course there were women and children, but they didn't count. Bird-in-Hand knew they would be outnumbered, probably about fifty to one, because the cavalry from Fort Crawford were sure to come to help the white men.

So for the next two days, the chief sat outside his teepee and planned his battle moves, while the braves got busy making arrows. They made as many arrows as they could, and they made them as strong and as swift and as sharp as they knew how to make them. Even though they didn't think Private Corcoran was much of a warrior, they wanted to be ready for him, especially if they were going to be outnumbered fifty to one.

Finally the third day dawned. With their brave chief Bird-in-Hand wearing his warbonnet and leading the way, they rode to the hill beside the creek. They could see that the white men

had built a little fort on top of the hill, but it didn't look like much of a fort to them.

When the chief signaled, the braves circled the fort, hid behind trees and bushes, and began to shoot. The cavalry did come, as the chief had figured it would, and the braves were outnumbered fifty to one. But they weren't afraid. They were skillful warriors, and almost every one of their arrows found its mark.

The white men weren't very good fighters, but there were so many of them that every once in a while one of their shots accidentally hit a brave. By the end of the day, six braves were too badly injured to go on fighting, and the creek ran red with their blood.

At sundown Chief Bird-in-Hand called the six remaining braves to him and said, "We are all that is left. If the white men knew how few of us there are, we would be at their mercy, so here is what we'll do."

Slowly and with great sadness, he took off his warbonnet and began pulling out all of the feathers. It was a magnificent headdress, the finest thing the chief had ever owned. It was made of hundreds of eagle feathers, and it was so long that it touched the ground in the back. Just putting on his warbonnet had always made the chief feel taller and braver and stronger. But now the bonnet was needed for something more important.

When he had finished pulling out all of the feathers, Bird-in-Hand divided them equally

among the six braves. "Go into the woods," he told them, "and find long sticks, as many as you can. Tie one feather to the top of each stick, then come back to me."

When the braves had done what he told them, they had a forest of feather-topped sticks.

"Now," the chief said, "spread out in a wide circle around the fort. Each of you build two or three campfires, so that the fort will be surrounded by the fires. Let them burn all night. The white men will see them, and be afraid. Then, at dawn," he said, pointing toward the east where the sun would be coming up, "place your sticks in the ground behind rocks and trees so that only the feathers show. The white men will think that under each feather is a warrior, and they will be afraid to go on fighting."

He raised his arm till he was pointing straight up. "When the sun is high in the heavens, I will go to the fort and give the white men a chance to surrender and make peace. If they believe they are surrounded by hundreds of our warriors, they will not fight. If they don't believe it, then we will all meet again in the Happy Hunting Ground."

"Won't you be afraid to go up to the fort?" one brave asked.

"No. I am your chief. I am not afraid of anything."

The braves nodded and disappeared into the darkness. Soon the campfires were lit, in a big circle around the fort. Bird-in-Hand smiled to himself at the sight of them. If he had not known better, he would have believed that the fort was surrounded by hundreds of braves.

Dawn came and the fires died out, but at the place where each fire had been, there were specks of white behind bushes, rocks, and tree trunks. As the sun rose higher, the men inside the fort could see that those specks of white were feathers of the kind that the Indians wore in their headbands.

Not a single shot was fired from the fort all morning, nor from the Indians. When the sun was high overhead, Chief Bird-in-Hand walked slowly toward the fort, waving a bit of white

cloth as a sign of peace and hoping the white
men wouldn't notice that he wasn't wearing his
warbonnet. The six warriors watched him from
their hiding places behind rocks and trees, and
they felt very proud of their chief. Bird-in-Hand
walked slowly, bravely, up to the fort.

Private Corcoran came outside to meet him.
"Your fort is surrounded by my braves," the

chief said, honestly enough. "I have come to give you a chance to make peace. My warriors and I do not wish to kill you or your people. Say that you will not put soapsuds in the creek, and we will let you live."

Private Corcoran thought it over, but not for long. Then he shook hands with the chief and thanked him for sparing the settlers' lives.

All the way back to their village, carrying their wounded, the braves shouted their praises of the wise and fearless chief Bird-in-Hand.

"We have the bravest chief of all," one man said. "We must honor him."

"We will make him a new warbonnet," said another.

A third brave said, "Yes. But that is not enough. We will name the place of the battle Bird-in-Hand Creek!"

But the chief smiled modestly and said, "No, that would be too bold. The gods might think I was proud, and punish us all."

"Then we won't give it your name," the brave answered. "We will just call it . . . Bravery Creek!"

And that was how Bravery Creek got its name.

Mr. Millering's Story

How Molly Corcoran Won a
Victory at Bravery Creek

When Johnnie was through telling his story,
Dennis didn't know what to think. He had
believed Orville, but now Johnnie's story seemed
just as true as the first one.

The two men sat staring at their fishing poles
in angry silence. It looked to Dennis as though
they wouldn't be speaking to each other for a
while.

Suddenly Mr. Millering spoke, "If you gentle-
men are interested in knowing what actually did
happen here at Bravery Creek, I think I can
help."

46

Orville and Johnnie stared in complete surprise at the well-dressed young man who had sat so quietly all afternoon.

"You?" said Orville rather rudely. "What in tunket could you tell us that we don't already know? After all, it was *my* great-grandfather who was the hero of it all."

"It was *my* great-grandfather," Johnnie Horsefeather insisted. "But Orville is right, for once. What would you know about it? You're a stranger here."

"Yes," Mr. Millering said politely, "I am a stranger here, but as you may know I came to Bravery Creek to study the local history. While I was doing that, I came across some very old letters, written by Captain Corcoran's wife, Molly. Actually, he was neither a captain nor a private. He was a corporal, which ranks in between."

"Captain," Orville growled.

And Johnnie said, "He was a private. Already I don't believe anything you're going to say."

Mr. Millering looked hurt. He quit talking and went back to fishing.

"Please tell us about the letters," Dennis pleaded. "I want to find out what really happened, even if they don't."

Mr. Millering brightened up again. Ignoring Orville and Johnnie, he turned toward Dennis.

"These were letters that Molly wrote to her parents and sisters back home in Ohio," he said. "She told them all about life on the frontier, and she described exactly how Bravery Creek got its name. Since you really want to know the truth, I'll tell you."

And this is the story that Mr. Millering told:

When the Corcorans and five other families came to settle beside the nameless little creek in Iowa, there was a great deal that had to be done right away. Cabins had to be built and firewood cut before winter came. The settlers also built fences and barns to keep their few cows and pigs safe through the winter, and they cut huge stacks of prairie grass for hay. Otherwise the stock would not have lived through the cold months. Some food was laid by for the settlers' families too, so they wouldn't starve before spring, when they could plant crops.

With all these necessities to take care of, the men didn't have time to dig wells beside each cabin. The creek was nearby, and for the time being they planned to get their water from it.

But one bright Monday morning, a few weeks after the settlers had arrived, Molly Corcoran said to her husband, "We have a problem. We're running out of clean clothes, and so are the other families."

Corporal Corcoran said, "Why don't you ladies do your washing over there in the creek, at that shallow place where the flat rocks are? You can rub the dirt out on the rocks and then spread the clothes on a tree limb to dry."

That sounded like a sensible idea to Molly, so she told the other wives. They took their laundry and their chunks of hog-fat soap and went to the shallow place where the clear creek water ran over moss-covered rocks.

No sooner had they started scrubbing and pounding than they heard loud splashing noises

from upstream, and all of a sudden the creek
water around their feet was very, very muddy.

Quickly Molly fished the corporal's red woolen
drawers out of the water, flung them over her
arm, and marched up the creek bank, just as
feisty as a little blue jay. What she saw as she
came around the bend made her pause, but only
for an instant.

It was half a dozen young Indian braves riding their ponies back and forth through the creek water, whooping and laughing and raising up a whole creekful of mud from the bottom of the water.

"Just what in Sam Hill do you think you're doing in our creek?" she demanded. "Don't you know this is Monday morning, and Monday is wash day? You're muddying our fresh water."

The Indians reined in their ponies and sat silently watching her. They scratched their heads and studied the way her lips were moving, but of course they couldn't understand her language. They knew she was angry, though, and they knew from the way she was standing up to them and scolding that this little red-haired woman was not afraid of them or anything else.

After a few minutes it occurred to Molly that, of course, the Indians couldn't understand English. She stopped talking and looked from one to the other until she figured out which one was the leader. It was Chief Bird-in-Hand. He was a very young chief at that time; in fact he had only been chiefing for a few months, and this was his very first run-in with anybody like Molly Corcoran.

Molly went up to his horse and began, slowly and patiently, to try to make the young chief understand her. She held up her husband's red winter drawers. She held up her bar of home-rendered hog-fat soap. She went over to the

creek and went through the motions of scrubbing. Then, whinnying and prancing like a pony, she splashed through the water till the mud rose to the surface. With a look of exaggerated sorrow, she pointed to the muddy water, to the Indians' ponies, and finally to the corporal's mud-streaked red drawers.

Chief Bird-in-Hand understood. He smiled and nodded to let her know that he understood, but then he frowned, scratched his head, and got down from his pony.

He pointed to the flies that were tormenting the ponies. Then, whinnying and prancing as Molly had done, he waded into the creek, splashed around like a pony, and came up smiling with pleasure, to show Molly that he was no longer bothered by the flies. Whinnying again, he got down on his hands and knees and drank from the creek water. Once again he came up smiling, this time to show he was no longer thirsty.

Thoughtfully, Molly sat down on a log to consider the problem. The chief sat down beside her and together, each in his own language, they thought about what to do. The flies droned, and the ponies' tails swished through the air while the two of them sat and thought. The creek water rippled and splashed with a sound that felt cool to Molly's ears.

After several minutes of thinking, Molly stood up and said, "I've got it!" Chief Bird-in-Hand didn't understand the words, but he must have understood the look of relief on Molly's face.

"Follow me," Molly said with a motion of her arm that included all of the braves. With the corporal's drawers over her arm and a line of Indian braves riding single file behind her, Molly marched back downstream to where the other wives were waiting.

"You use this place," she said to the chief with much pointing and gesturing so he would know what she meant, "and we'll go upstream to do our washing. That way, your mud will float down that way, away from where we are."

The chief nodded and smiled, and the two groups exchanged places.

At first Molly felt smug as she went back to her scrubbing. She told the other wives how easy it is to handle Indians once you get the knack of it. She was so proud of herself that she didn't notice that the red dye from the corporal's drawers was making the creek water red, and that all of the soap they were using was sending billowy clouds of suds down the creek toward the Indians' ponies.

But before she'd started on her next piece of laundry, there was a huge splashing and neighing from downstream and a sudden sound of ponies galloping away.

"I guess they finished watering their horses," Molly started to say, but one of the other wives gave a scream. Molly turned around.

Behind her stood Chief Bird-in-Hand. His arms were crossed over his chest, his eyes were shooting lightning flashes down at her, and he was dripping wet. Even the eagle feather in his hair was drooping and dripping and thoroughly bedraggled.

"Oh, dear," Molly said. The other wives grabbed up their laundry and turned and ran for the safety of their cabins.

The chief glowered down at her for what seemed to be several years and an eternity. Then he stalked over to the creek. He pointed down at the red water with its foam of soapsuds.

Whinnying to show that he was a pony, he pretended to drink the red, soapy water, then made a horrible face, stuck out his tongue and said, "Ugh!"

Sadly Molly nodded her head in agreement, and again the two of them sat down on the log to think it over. While Molly and the chief pondered, the other braves had gone running off through the long prairie grass, trying to catch their ponies.

Suddenly the chief stood up and said something or other in his language. Molly didn't understand the words, but she figured from the look on his face that he had thought of something.

He pointed to the sun, and then moved his arm till he was pointing directly up at the center of the sky. From there he motioned to the east with one hand while he made scrubbing motions with the other hand. Then, pausing to let that part sink in, he pointed from the middle of the sky to the west and made whinnying, slurping sounds.

Molly stared at him, puzzled.

He went through the motions again, more slowly this time.

Molly was beginning to feel stupid. She shrugged helplessly, so he went through the motions a third time.

Suddenly she understood. "Oh, yes," she said, laughing with relief. "You mean we can have the creek in the mornings, and you'll have it in the afternoons. That's a wonderful idea. I was just about to think of it myself." With a grin spreading over her pretty freckled face, Molly stepped up to the chief and shook his hand.

Just then the corporal came crashing through the bushes, his face white with fear. He stopped in his tracks when he saw Molly standing there shaking hands with an Indian. But it didn't take long for him to see that it was a friendly handshake and that Molly was smiling.

"What in thunder is going on here, Molly? I was building the corral fence a little ways down the creek, and all of a sudden I noticed that the creek water was as red as blood. Just

then a whole tribe of Indians went whooping off through the grass. It scared the daylights out of me. I remembered you and the other ladies were up here washing clothes, and I was afraid the Indians might have hurt you."

Molly gave the chief a last friendly little pat on the arm, then went to stand beside her husband.

"It was nothing like that at all," she said, grinning at the chief. "I was just having a little discussion with the chief here. We had a bit of a problem, but it's all taken care of now. Good-bye, chief."

She waved, and the chief waved, and they went their separate ways.

That night after supper Molly told the corporal all about the agreement, and he promised to tell all the other families not to do their laundry in the afternoons.

"You know, Molly, that was a very brave thing you did today," he said, smiling down at her with pride in his eyes. "If you hadn't used your head and settled this little problem with the Indians, it might easily have grown into a much bigger problem, maybe even a war."

She waved him away, but she couldn't help looking a little bit proud herself.

"In fact," the corporal went on, "I'm going to suggest to the others that we name this place in honor of you. How would you like that?"

She thought about it. "Molly Creek? Sounds kind of silly, if you ask me."

The corporal laughed. "No, not Molly Creek. Bravery Creek, because of the way you stood up to the Indians when most women would have run screaming for home."

Molly thought for a moment, then smiled and said simply, "I'd like that."

And that is the true story of the famous battle of Bravery Creek.

Or is it?

MEET THE AUTHOR

In a century-old farmhouse in northeast Iowa, LYNN HALL turns out delightful books for children. A desire for personal freedom and a wish to live in the country led her to quit her job at an ad agency and take up writing which, she says, gives her a "meaningful, rewarding, and creative life style." Before becoming an author, Miss Hall had an interesting variety of jobs from professional dog handler to secretary. Her hobbies include breeding and showing cocker spaniels, riding horseback, and learning to play the piano. In addition, she is a counselor for teenagers in trouble.

MEET THE ARTIST

HERMAN B. VESTAL loves both painting and the sea. Before studying art at the National Academy of Design and at the Pratt Institute, he went to sea in the Merchant Marine. During World War II he served in the Coast Guard as a combat artist. His assignments included recording the Normandy landing and the invasion of Iwo Jima. Today, his interest in the sea continues through his hobby—sailboat racing. Primarily a book illustrator, Mr. Vestal also enjoys doing watercolors and is a member of the American Watercolor Society. Mr. Vestal, his wife, and son live in Little Silver, New Jersey.